The Symbion Alphabet

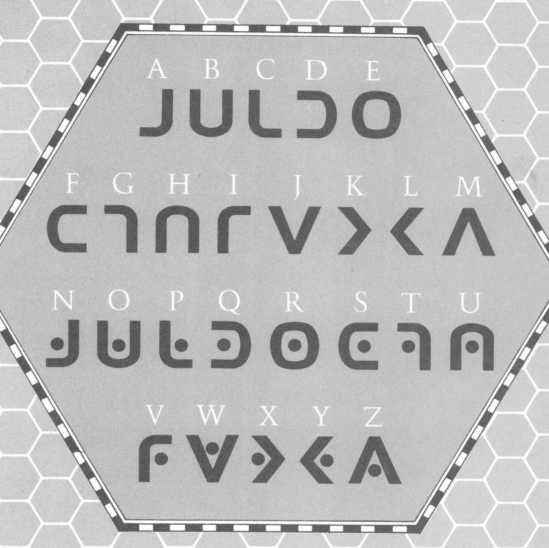

SECRET IN THE VALLEY OF MEANDER

Written by Sonia Black   Illustrated by Steven Geiger and Roberta Edelman

Prince Dargon was having fun skyriding on his insectoid, DragonFlyer. Dargon would someday be king of the Shining Realm on the planet Symbion. Dargon looked below and saw a group of Sectaurs and insectoids entering Symbator, the Citadel of Power.

"I'm afraid the fun's over," he said to DragonFlyer. "Duty calls. It's time for the special meeting I called at the castle."

DragonFlyer made one swift swoop towards the castle. Dargon dismounted and went to the meeting.

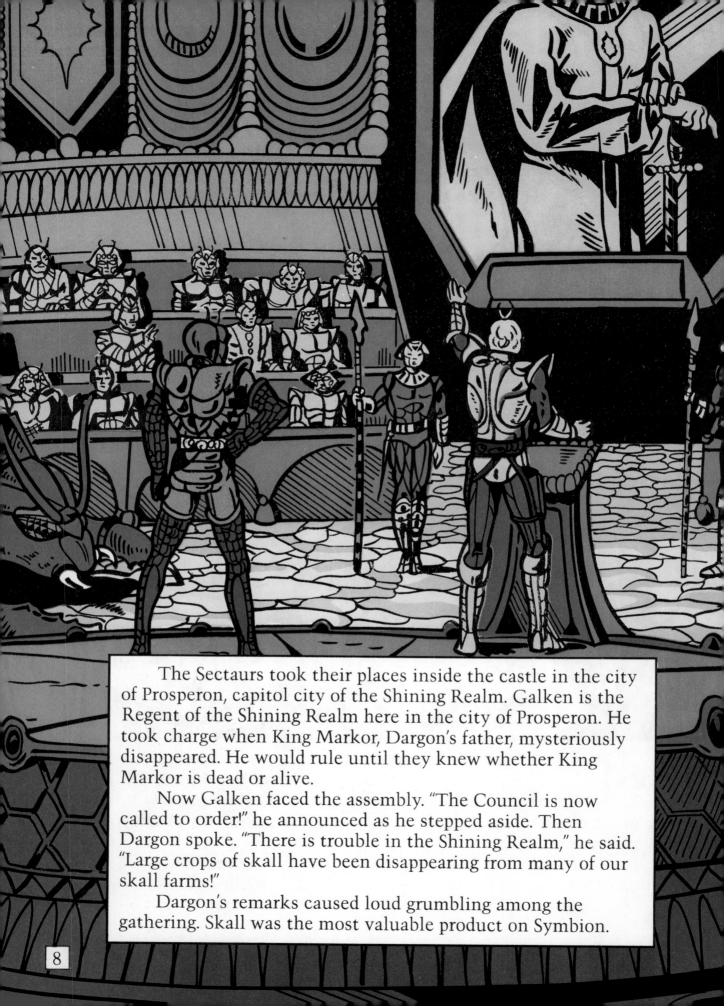

The Sectaurs took their places inside the castle in the city of Prosperon, capitol city of the Shining Realm. Galken is the Regent of the Shining Realm here in the city of Prosperon. He took charge when King Markor, Dargon's father, mysteriously disappeared. He would rule until they knew whether King Markor is dead or alive.

Now Galken faced the assembly. "The Council is now called to order!" he announced as he stepped aside. Then Dargon spoke. "There is trouble in the Shining Realm," he said. "Large crops of skall have been disappearing from many of our skall farms!"

Dargon's remarks caused loud grumbling among the gathering. Skall was the most valuable product on Symbion.

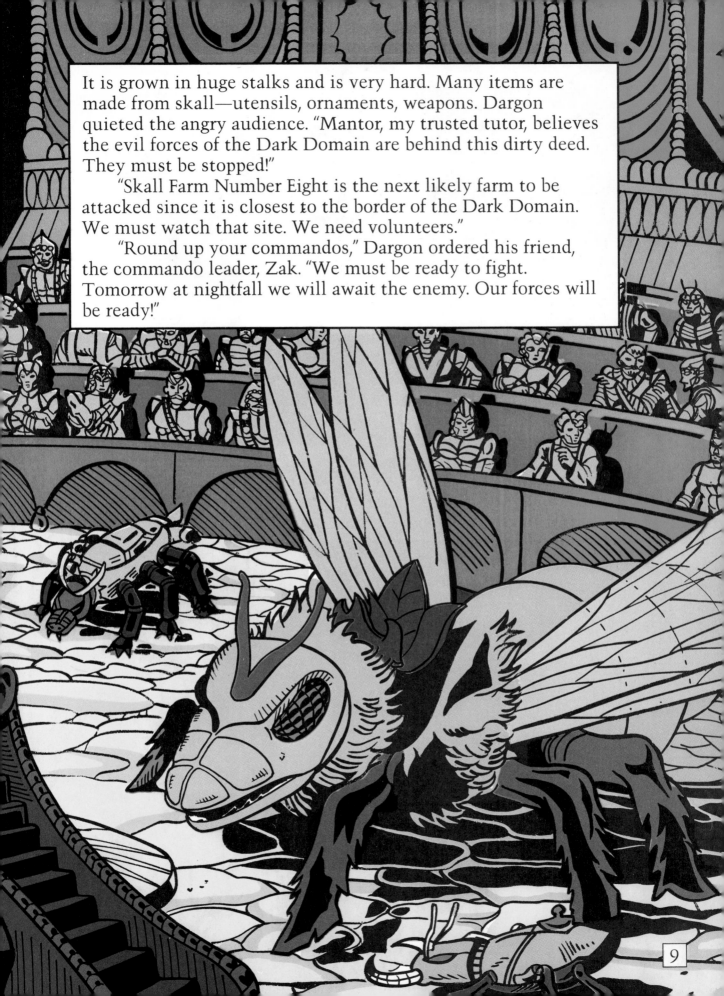

It is grown in huge stalks and is very hard. Many items are made from skall—utensils, ornaments, weapons. Dargon quieted the angry audience. "Mantor, my trusted tutor, believes the evil forces of the Dark Domain are behind this dirty deed. They must be stopped!"

"Skall Farm Number Eight is the next likely farm to be attacked since it is closest to the border of the Dark Domain. We must watch that site. We need volunteers."

"Round up your commandos," Dargon ordered his friend, the commando leader, Zak. "We must be ready to fight. Tomorrow at nightfall we will await the enemy. Our forces will be ready!"

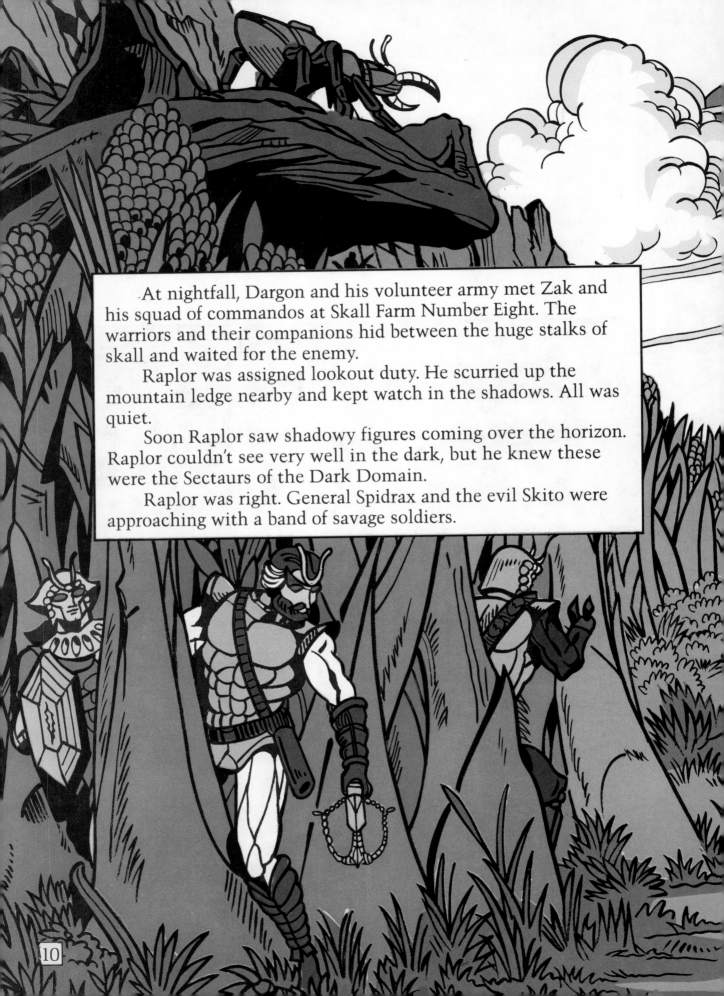

At nightfall, Dargon and his volunteer army met Zak and his squad of commandos at Skall Farm Number Eight. The warriors and their companions hid between the huge stalks of skall and waited for the enemy.

Raplor was assigned lookout duty. He scurried up the mountain ledge nearby and kept watch in the shadows. All was quiet.

Soon Raplor saw shadowy figures coming over the horizon. Raplor couldn't see very well in the dark, but he knew these were the Sectaurs of the Dark Domain.

Raplor was right. General Spidrax and the evil Skito were approaching with a band of savage soldiers.

From his hiding place, Mantor sensed his insectoid companion, Raplor, was on to something. The Sectaurs and their insectoid companions have a special psychic bond. They can communicate silently. This is called telebonding.

In an instant, Raplor sent Mantor this silent message: *The enemy is approaching!* Mantor quietly relayed the information to his comrades. They were ready for action!

The battle was on! But General Spidrax and his army were not caught by surprise. SpiderFlyer had warned them about the ambush!

SpiderFlyer has many eyes so he can see at great distances and in all directions! SpiderFlyer spotted Dargon and his army in their hiding places from very far away.

"Should we retreat, General?" Skito had asked.

"Never!" bellowed General Spidrax. "Advance!" Skito let out a chilling laugh as they sped to battle.

Spidrax and Dargon met head on. Spidrax lashed at Dargon with his venom-tipped whip, but the whip missed its mark.

Dargon's aim was right on target. The poison dart from his vengun hit Spidrax in the arm. Instantly, Spidrax slumped over unconscious on SpiderFlyer.

SpiderFlyer was enraged. He shot out his venom-coated web at Dargon, but that missed too. The poisonous material dropped onto some of SpiderFlyer's own troops and the savage soldiers were knocked unconscious. SpiderFlyer saw he was losing and flew off, carrying the unconscious Spidrax with him.

Skito was in a heated duel with Zak. Skito saw his soldiers falling and started to back off. "Retreat!" he called out. "We're being outnumbered! Retreat!"

"Follow them!" Dargon ordered his troops. "They could lead us to the stolen skall!"

Skito and his evil gang quickly vanished into the dark night. Only Toxcid was still in sight as he swiftly scrambled over the rough territory. Bitaur stealthily followed close behind. Dargon, Zak, Mantor, and Pinsor and their insectoids stayed farther back. Where was Toxcid headed?

After traveling many miles, they could vaguely see the sinister castle of the Empress Devora in the distance. "Grimhold Castle!" Zak gasped.

"We're in Synax!" Dargon exclaimed. Synax is the largest city in the Dark Domain.

"Enemy territory!" said Pinsor.

"We must be extra careful now," Mantor advised.

"Indeed!" Dargon replied.

"If Toxcid goes into the castle, so must we," Dargon declared. "We have a mission to complete. We must find out what we can about the stolen skall!"

Toxcid finally reached Grimhold Castle. He showed no fear because he had no idea he was being followed.

Meanwhile, Dargon and Zak crept closer to the castle's entrance. The two brave warriors would enter the terrifying castle alone!

Pinsor, Dargon's loyal warrior, objected. "I should accompany you, Dargon!" he said.

"No, trusted one," Dargon replied. "You keep watch with the others."

"Be careful!" Pinsor warned. Dargon and Zak crept closer still to the castle while the other heroes kept watch. Raplor scuttled up a tree for a better view.

17

Horrors! Toxcid noticed that Dargon and Zak were following him. He scrambled into the underbrush. "Where did he go?" asked Zak.

Zak soon found out. Toxcid came up behind them and began spouting venom from his snout. Dargon swung his broadskall, but he had to keep dodging to avoid Toxcid's spurts of deadly venom.

From his spot in the treetop, Raplor was the first to see that Zak and Dargon were in terrible danger. Before anyone else could act, Raplor let out his extra long appendage. He extended it farther and farther. In a flash, it grabbed Toxcid by the neck. Toxcid was so shocked that he stopped shooting his venom. He thrashed his legs around, trying to escape, but Raplor held him tightly.

Dargon moved quickly. He and Zak ran toward Grimhold Castle. They were now approaching the entrance.

"Are you sure you want to continue this mission?" Dargon asked. "It's going to be even more dangerous."

"Let's go!" said Zak.

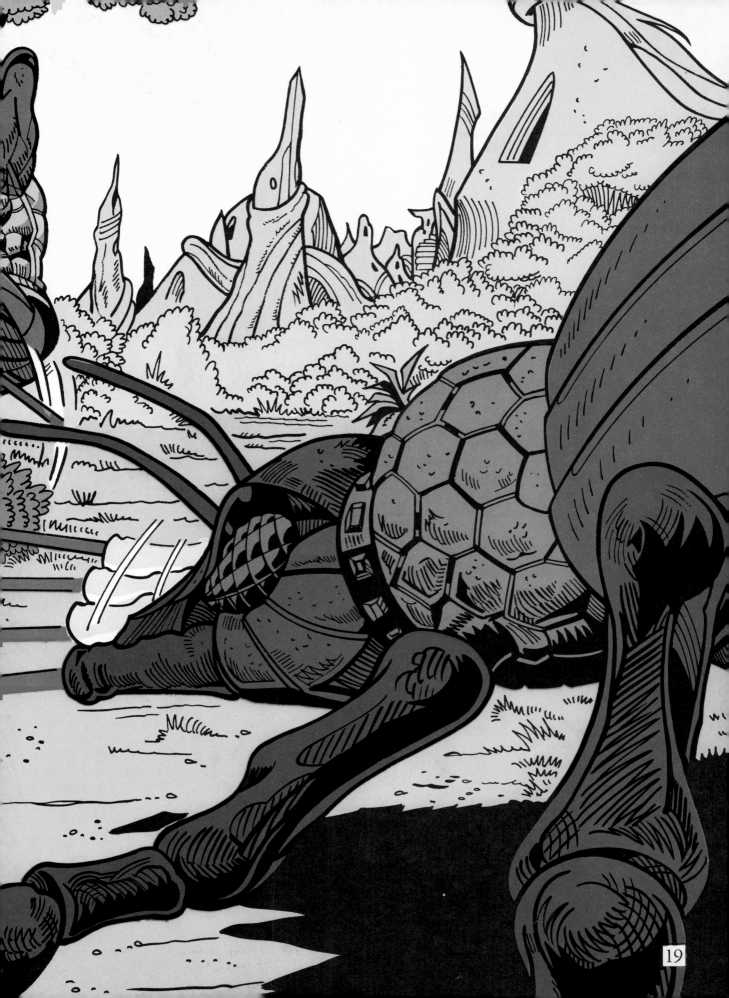

Dargon and Zak heard loud talking inside Grimhold Castle.

They tiptoed silently in the direction of the voices—toward the Empress' meeting chamber. The Empress Devora is the ruler of the Dark Domain.

Dargon and Zak stood stiffly up against the wall outside the door. They listened closely. The two soon found out that the villains had indeed fled to Grimhold. General Spidrax and Skito were among those inside. The Empress Devora was demanding an explanation for their actions.

"Fools! You fools!" she repeated. "Why did you knowingly walk right into a set up?

"Soldiers!" Commander Waspax's voice boomed. "That mission should have been simple!"

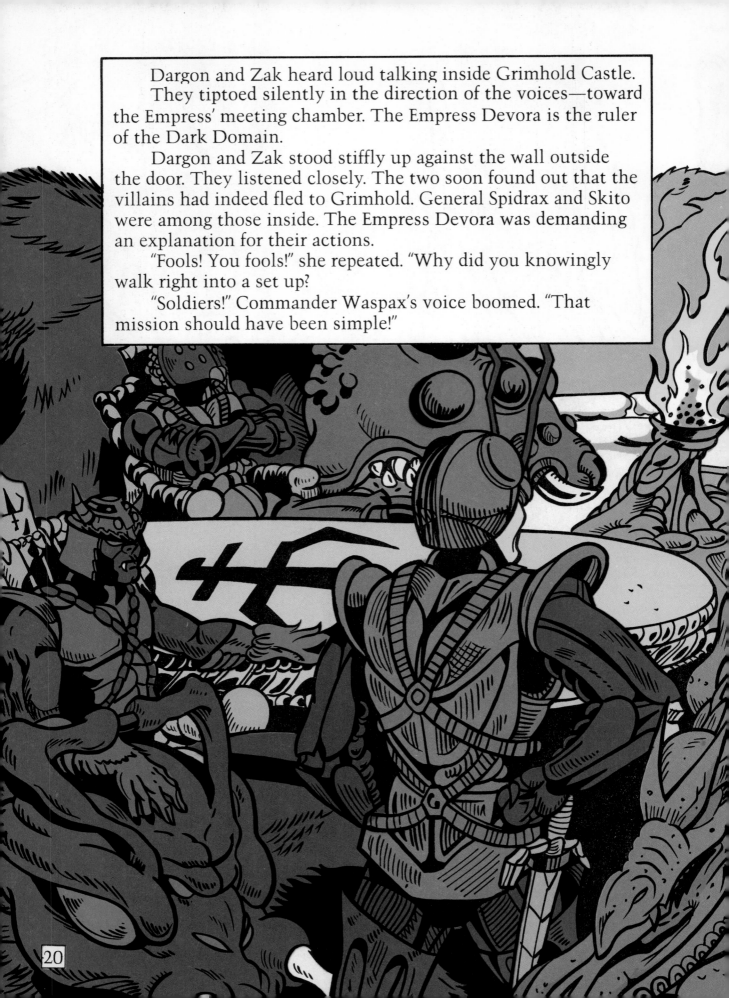

"Quiet!" commanded Devora. "We must form another plan to secure that skall crop. We need every stalk to complete the secret skall fortress in the Valley of Meander. Once the mighty fortress is done, we will lure the forces of the Shining Realm to the site. They will be powerless against us in that super structure and the Shining Realm will be ours!"

Dargon and Zak looked at each other in shock. Now everything was clear.

Suddenly, footsteps approached from behind. There was nowhere to run.

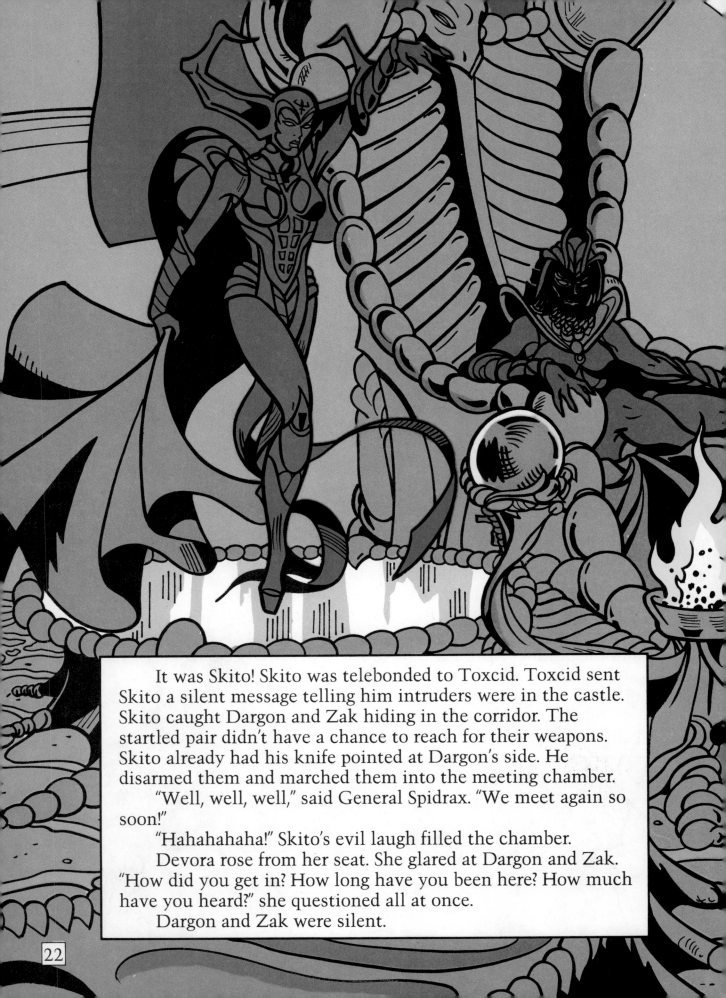

It was Skito! Skito was telebonded to Toxcid. Toxcid sent Skito a silent message telling him intruders were in the castle. Skito caught Dargon and Zak hiding in the corridor. The startled pair didn't have a chance to reach for their weapons. Skito already had his knife pointed at Dargon's side. He disarmed them and marched them into the meeting chamber.

"Well, well, well," said General Spidrax. "We meet again so soon!"

"Hahahahaha!" Skito's evil laugh filled the chamber.

Devora rose from her seat. She glared at Dargon and Zak. "How did you get in? How long have you been here? How much have you heard?" she questioned all at once.

Dargon and Zak were silent.

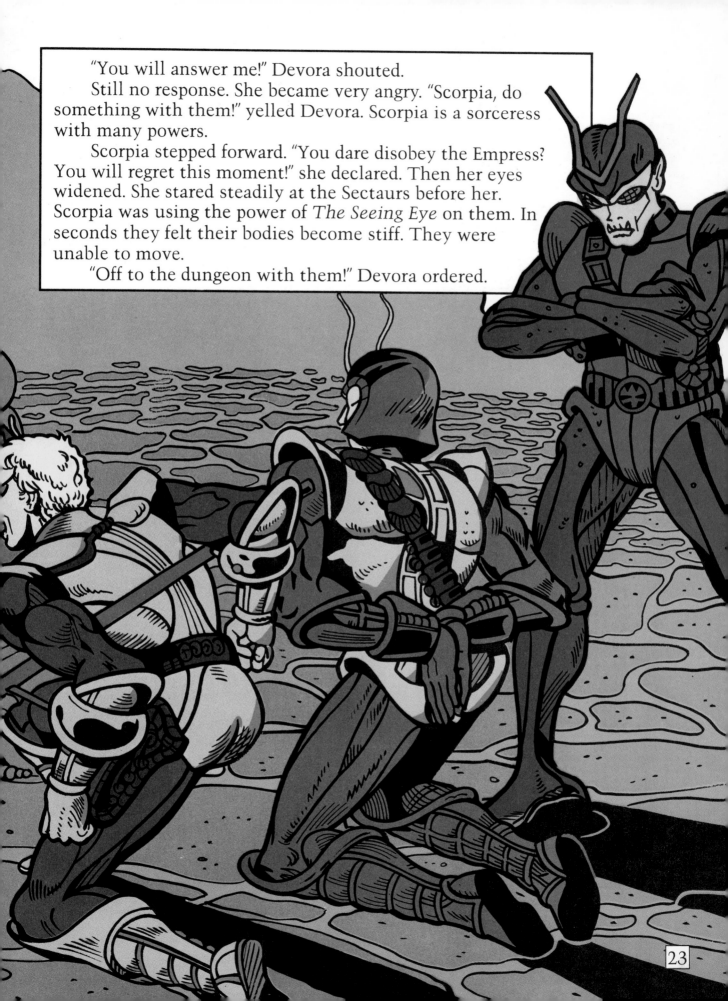

"You will answer me!" Devora shouted.

Still no response. She became very angry. "Scorpia, do something with them!" yelled Devora. Scorpia is a sorceress with many powers.

Scorpia stepped forward. "You dare disobey the Empress? You will regret this moment!" she declared. Then her eyes widened. She stared steadily at the Sectaurs before her. Scorpia was using the power of *The Seeing Eye* on them. In seconds they felt their bodies become stiff. They were unable to move.

"Off to the dungeon with them!" Devora ordered.

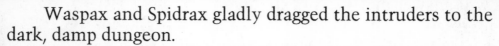

Waspax and Spidrax gladly dragged the intruders to the dark, damp dungeon.

Waspax stood back and looked at the stiff figures. He looked around the gloomy cellar. "Aah! All the comforts of home," he chuckled.

Spidrax snickered at them, "Where are your brave soldiers now when you need their help?"

The warriors were in a trance-like state. There was no way they could let their friends know they needed assistance. They were helpless against their enemy.

Little did they know, help *was* on the way!

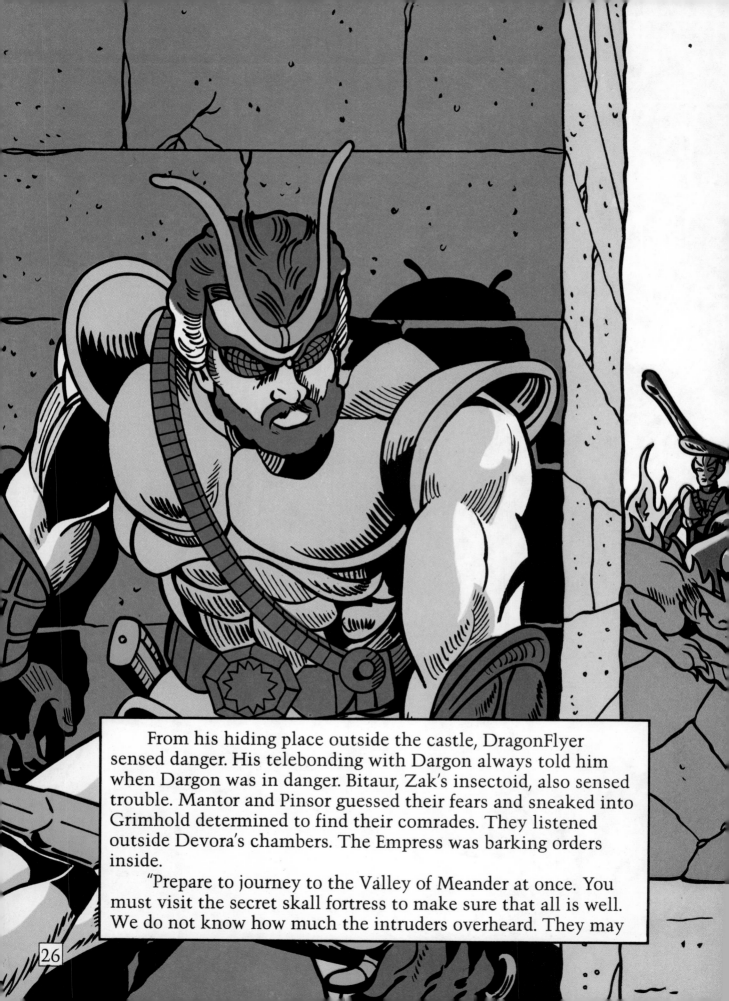

From his hiding place outside the castle, DragonFlyer sensed danger. His telebonding with Dargon always told him when Dargon was in danger. Bitaur, Zak's insectoid, also sensed trouble. Mantor and Pinsor guessed their fears and sneaked into Grimhold determined to find their comrades. They listened outside Devora's chambers. The Empress was barking orders inside.

"Prepare to journey to the Valley of Meander at once. You must visit the secret skall fortress to make sure that all is well. We do not know how much the intruders overheard. They may

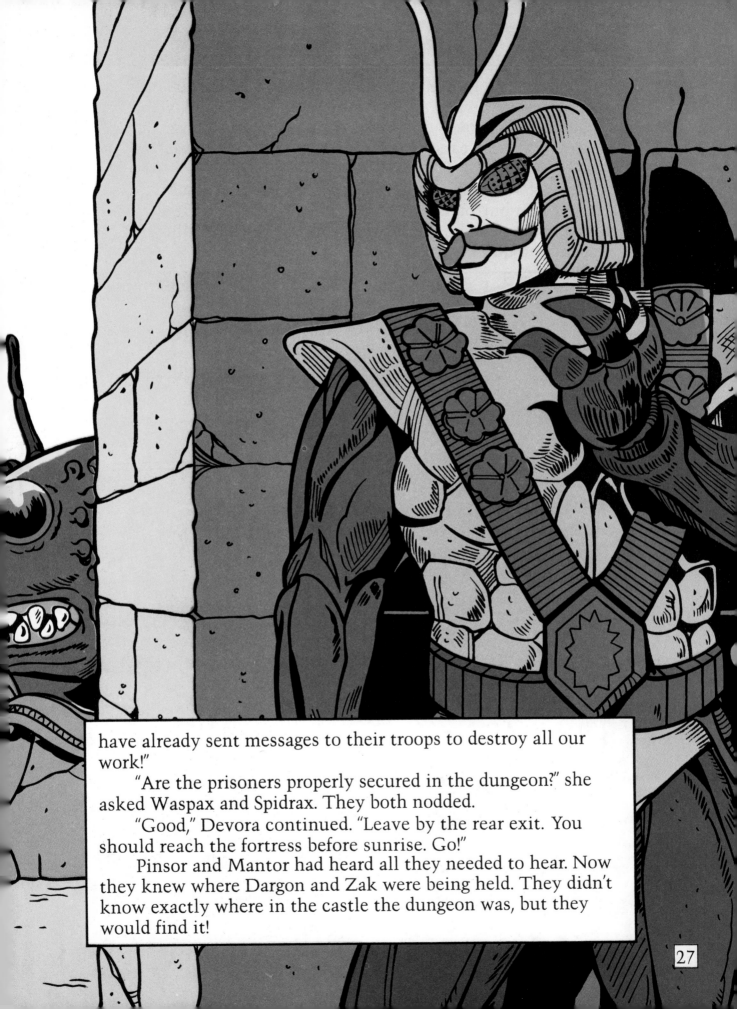

have already sent messages to their troops to destroy all our work!"

"Are the prisoners properly secured in the dungeon?" she asked Waspax and Spidrax. They both nodded.

"Good," Devora continued. "Leave by the rear exit. You should reach the fortress before sunrise. Go!"

Pinsor and Mantor had heard all they needed to hear. Now they knew where Dargon and Zak were being held. They didn't know exactly where in the castle the dungeon was, but they would find it!

Mantor and Pinsor headed straight for the other end of the corridor where there was a staircase. Maybe it would lead to the dungeon. They moved quickly and quietly. Pinsor sensed a new danger! He couldn't tell what it was, but he knew it was very close.

It was! The corridor was loaded with booby traps. Mantor stepped on a button-like object on the floor and suddenly a gaping hole opened under his feet! He felt himself falling fast! It happened so quickly, there was nothing he could do!

Pinsor reached after Mantor and tripped. He grabbed onto the wall to steady himself. His big claws hit a hidden button on the wall. From out of nowhere, a heavy net fell over him. It pinned him to the floor! Pinsor held the net in his massive claws. With his incredible strength, he burst free from the trap.

Pinsor looked down the hole where Mantor had disappeared. He saw nothing but darkness! Where does it lead? he wondered. There was no time to think. He had to find Mantor. Pinsor climbed over the edge of the opening. He fell down, down the gloomy black hole!

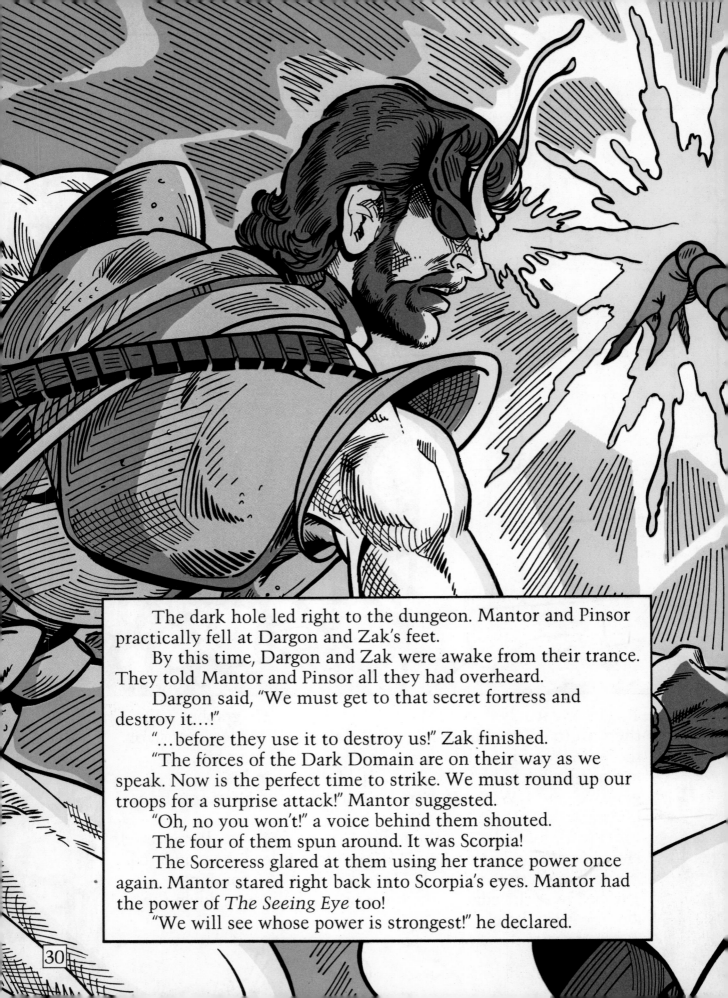

The dark hole led right to the dungeon. Mantor and Pinsor practically fell at Dargon and Zak's feet.

By this time, Dargon and Zak were awake from their trance. They told Mantor and Pinsor all they had overheard.

Dargon said, "We must get to that secret fortress and destroy it...!"

"...before they use it to destroy us!" Zak finished.

"The forces of the Dark Domain are on their way as we speak. Now is the perfect time to strike. We must round up our troops for a surprise attack!" Mantor suggested.

"Oh, no you won't!" a voice behind them shouted.

The four of them spun around. It was Scorpia!

The Sorceress glared at them using her trance power once again. Mantor stared right back into Scorpia's eyes. Mantor had the power of *The Seeing Eye* too!

"We will see whose power is strongest!" he declared.

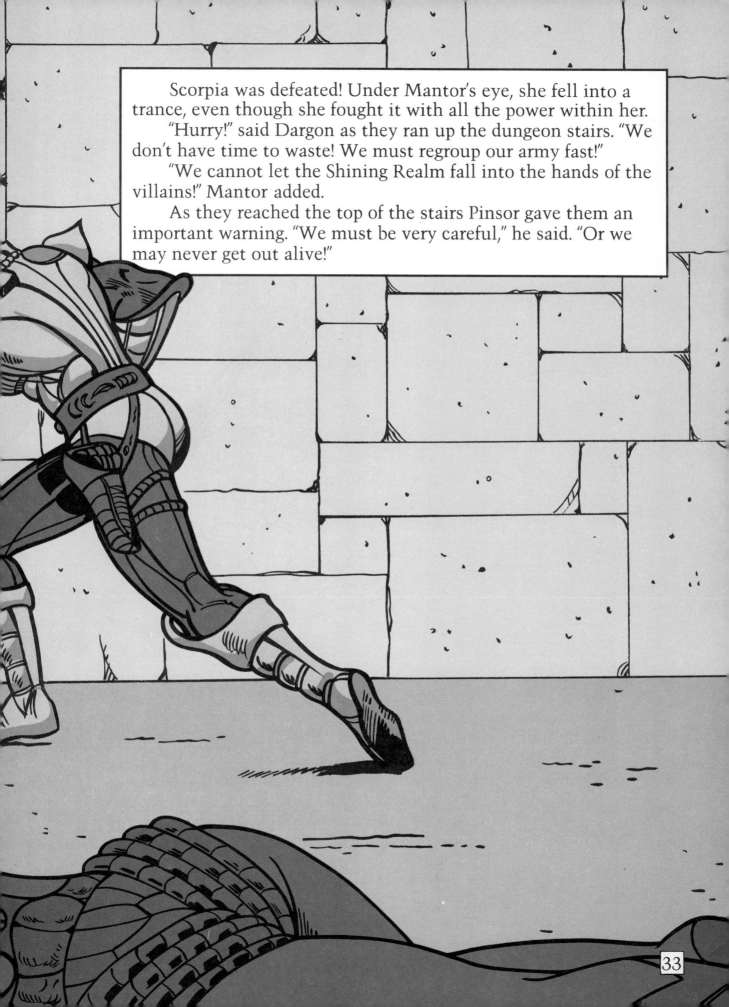

Scorpia was defeated! Under Mantor's eye, she fell into a trance, even though she fought it with all the power within her.

"Hurry!" said Dargon as they ran up the dungeon stairs. "We don't have time to waste! We must regroup our army fast!"

"We cannot let the Shining Realm fall into the hands of the villains!" Mantor added.

As they reached the top of the stairs Pinsor gave them an important warning. "We must be very careful," he said. "Or we may never get out alive!"

Pinsor was right! They reached the castle entrance safely, but suddenly, they heard a noise behind them. The four froze! Two giant monsters were charging towards them snapping their hungry jaws!

Dargon quickly flashed a telebond message to DragonFlyer for help. In an instant, the insectoid swooped down by the castle door. Dargon and Zak jumped onto DragonFlyer's back. Pinsor and Mantor clung to the back of DragonFlyer's saddle and the courageous insectoid carried them all to safety. Then DragonFlyer fled swiftly to the city of Prosperon to sound the alarm.

It was almost dawn. The warriors and their companions anxiously waited for DragonFlyer's return with the troops.

In no time DragonFlyer and the mighty army of the Shining Realm approached. Dargon and the others quickly joined them.

"Well done, DragonFlyer!" Dargon said to his swift insectoid. Then he turned to the soldiers. "Troops, advance!" he ordered.

The troops proceeded in the direction of the Valley of Meander. "Commander Waspax and General Spidrax will be expecting us," Zak said. "We must move quickly to surround their skall fortress. We will use every means we have to capture that stronghold. We have some advantage since we can see through the fog, Meander, and they can't."

Dargon and his army attacked the enemy fortress, but the enemy was ready and waiting for their arrival. The villains were inside the mighty fortress. They returned fire for fire. Dargon's soldiers took cover. They kept firing but their weapons just bounced off the fortress wall.

Battle Beetle rushed at the door. He tried to rip it apart with his powerful claws. The door wouldn't budge.

"Surrender your forces, Dargon. You cannot win!" Commander Waspax shouted from inside.

"Never!" Dargon shouted back. But it seemed hopeless!

Zak climbed to the roof of the fortress. He aimed his slazor gun down the chimney opening and fired furiously. Instantly, the sound of repeated explosions rang out!

The doors of the fortress suddenly swung wide open. A thick black smoke poured out. Spidrax, Waspax, and their evil forces came charging out. Some of their warriors were being carried out. They were all overcome by the smoke, coughing nonstop. Behind them flames leaped inside the fortress.

"We surrender!" Skito shouted between coughs. He waved a white flag.

The pellets Zak fired from his slazor gun had done the trick. The pellets were filled with gas. When they struck, they exploded instantly. Sparks from the explosion started a raging fire inside the fortress. The evil Sectaurs could not take the intense heat. And the gas fumes the pellets released helped to drive them out.

Now their fate was in Dargon's hands!

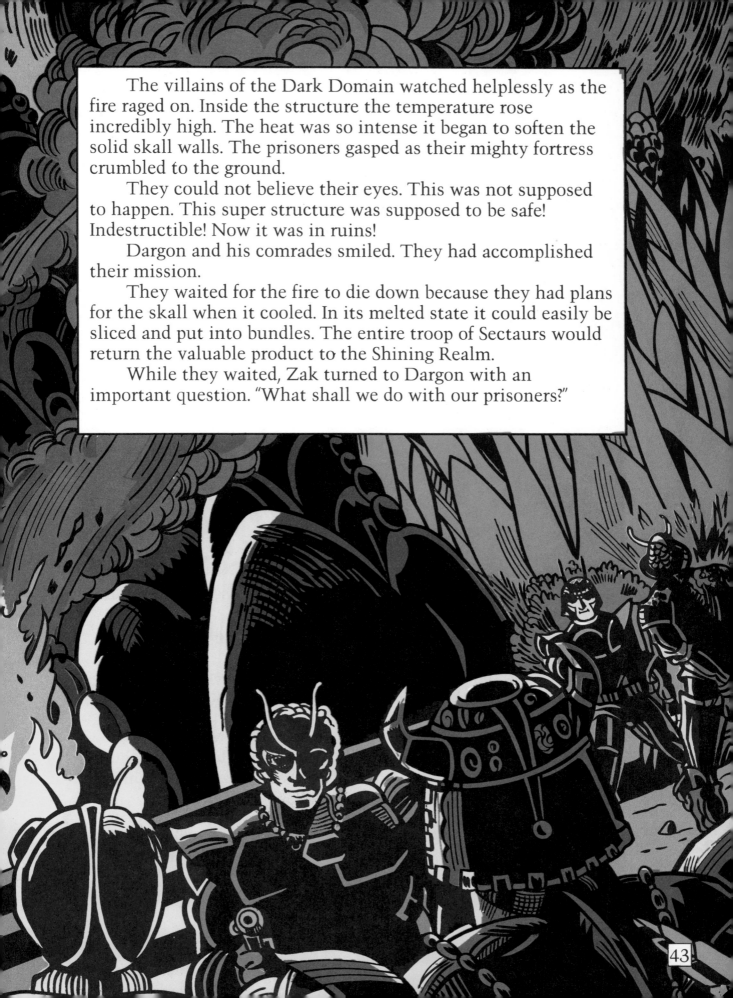

The villains of the Dark Domain watched helplessly as the fire raged on. Inside the structure the temperature rose incredibly high. The heat was so intense it began to soften the solid skall walls. The prisoners gasped as their mighty fortress crumbled to the ground.

They could not believe their eyes. This was not supposed to happen. This super structure was supposed to be safe! Indestructible! Now it was in ruins!

Dargon and his comrades smiled. They had accomplished their mission.

They waited for the fire to die down because they had plans for the skall when it cooled. In its melted state it could easily be sliced and put into bundles. The entire troop of Sectaurs would return the valuable product to the Shining Realm.

While they waited, Zak turned to Dargon with an important question. "What shall we do with our prisoners?"

Dargon thought about Zak's question for a second. Then he answered, "Our prisoners are free to go!"

The enemy troops were surprised. They couldn't believe their ears.

Then Dargon continued. "They will have to suffer the punishment of the Empress Devora! Once they return with the news of the fallen fortress, she will deal with them harshly!"

Spidrax and Waspax were filled with mixed feelings. They were happy to be released but they did not look forward to their meeting with the Empress. They knew Dargon was right. They knew what Devora's reaction would be.

They rounded up their troops and headed back to the Dark Domain—soundly defeated. Before they crossed over the horizon, Spidrax yelled out, "We'll meet again, Dargon! Next time you will not be so lucky!"

His words echoed across the valley. Dargon answered softly, "We will see about that, Spidrax! We will see!"

SKALL
ISLAND

LAKE OF BLOOD

THE
DARK DOMAIN

SEA OF ACID RAIN

THE SHINING
REALM

BLUE FOREST
OF FORGETFULNESS

CITY
OF ANCIENTS

THE
DEADLY
SWAMP

DESERT
OF LOST HOPE

MOUNT
SECTAUR

FOG OF MEANDER

(AREA BEYOND HEXAGON BORDER IS THE FORBIDDEN ZONE)

The Land of Symbion